My Bestest Wish ever

Written by: Peggy Barber
Illustrated by: Misty Hawthorne
Narrated by: Pickles the Pig

To order additional copies of this book, contact:
Xlibris
844-714-8691
www.Xlibris.com
Orders@Xlibris.com

Library of Congress Control Number: 2022921848
ISBN: Softcover   978-1-6698-5695-5
          Hardcover   978-1-6698-5696-2
          EBook   978-1-6698-5697-9

Library of Congress Control Number: 2022921848

Print information available on the last page

Rev. date: 12/16/2022

My Bestest
Wish ever

Have you ever wished for something you did not have? Seeing it in your mind? Just knowing it would be the best wish that could ever happen to you? Have you? Have you ever done that??? Well. . .

Then let me tell how it was the day I got my most wished for wish!

My name is Pickles and I'm a Pig. I live in a little pen. I long to be free to run in the big yard and play with Popsicle, he's a puppy, "YEAH"

and Poppy, she's a girl,

"YUCK"

One day Mr. Pumpernickel, he's Poppy's dad, did not come to feed me like he always does. Today was different BECAUSE . . .

Poppy came to feed me by herself. She was carrying my food in a hat. But instead of giving me my food in my pan, she put it down on the ground outside my pen. Mr. Pumpernickel never does that!

I looked at my food outside my pen. I tried to wait for Poppy to put my food in my pan. I really did! But she was not there. She had run away!

I looked for Mr. Pumpernickel or Poppy to come and put my food in my pan, so I could eat. I looked and I looked. I was trying so hard to be good and stay in my pen, but my hungry tummy got the better of me.

Well, what would you do if you were me?

My food was not in my pan where it should be.

The gate was not closed as it should be.

My food was outside the pen where it should not be.

I was still hungry as I should not be.

Well I wanted my food. I was really hungry. Have you ever been really, really hungry? So hungry you just couldn't wait? Just had to have it? Do you understand? Do you understand what happened next?

I stepped through the gate and what did I see? I saw a Great Big Yard and I was FREE!!!

FREE to play! FREE to run! This was my best wish of all wishes. My BESTEST WISH ever come true!

Suddenly, I wasn't hungry at all!

I ran and I frolicked all over the yard. I looked for Popsicle and Poppy. I waited for them to come and play, to share my BESTEST WISH ever.

I wanted to find Popsicle and Poppy. Well, maybe not Poppy, She's a girl, but Popsicle only comes outside when Poppy's outside. I guess he needs a puppy sitter. Why don't I need a pig sitter?

Is it because I'm just a pig who lives in a small pen with no room to run and play, or maybe run away?

Is that what Popsicle would do, run away, if he didn't have Poppy to play with too?

All of a sudden, out of the house came Popsicle, Poppy and Mr. Pumpernickel! All running toward me calling my name.

They scared me so bad I ran down the driveway as fast as I could, but my fastest fast was not fast enough! Popsicle ran past me, barking at me. Not like a friend at all.

I was so afraid I spun around and ran back up the driveway as fast as I could! Past Mr. Pumpernickel! Past Poppy too!

Back to my little pen. My little pen that I had wished so hard to get out of. Finding out that my BESTEST WISH ever was to be in my little pen after all.

THE END

Create Your Own Story of Your Bestest Wish Ever

Create Your Own Story of Your Bestest Wish Ever

Create Your Own Story of Your Bestest Wish Ever

Create Your Own Story of Your Bestest Wish Ever

Create Your Own Story of Your Bestest Wish Ever

Printed in the United States
by Baker & Taylor Publisher Services